Sheep Trick or Treat

Nancy Shaw

Sheep Trick or Treat

illustrated by Margot Apple

SCHOLASTIC INC.
New York Toronto London Auckland Sydney
Mexico City New Delhi Hong Kong

For Margot
— N.S.

For Jack Werner and Pixie Lauer
and all the kids at the Harbor Children's Center
— M.A.

ISBN 0-439-13347-5

Published by Scholastic Inc., 555 Broadway, New York, NY 10012,
by arrangement with Houghton Mifflin Company.

12 11 10 9 8 7 6 5 4 3 2 1 9/9 0 1 2 3 4/0

Printed in the U.S.A. 24

First Scholastic printing, September 1999

The text of this book is set in 24 point Garamond 3.
The illustrations colored pencil, reproduced in full color.

As the Halloween moon rises,

Sheep are fixing up disguises.

They make a mask with glue and tape

And a monster suit with a shiny cape.

Sheep snip and sew and drape

A costume for a giant ape.

Sheep shape wool in pointy clumps

To make a dinosaur with bumps.

Sheep rip scraps for mummy wraps.

Sheep pose in spooky clothes.

Sheep take lanterns. Arm in arm,

They set off for a nearby farm.

In the woods, they give three cheers.

A sleepy wolf perks up his ears.

Sheep amble to the dell.

They reach the barn and ring the bell.

Sheep bleat. Trick or treat!

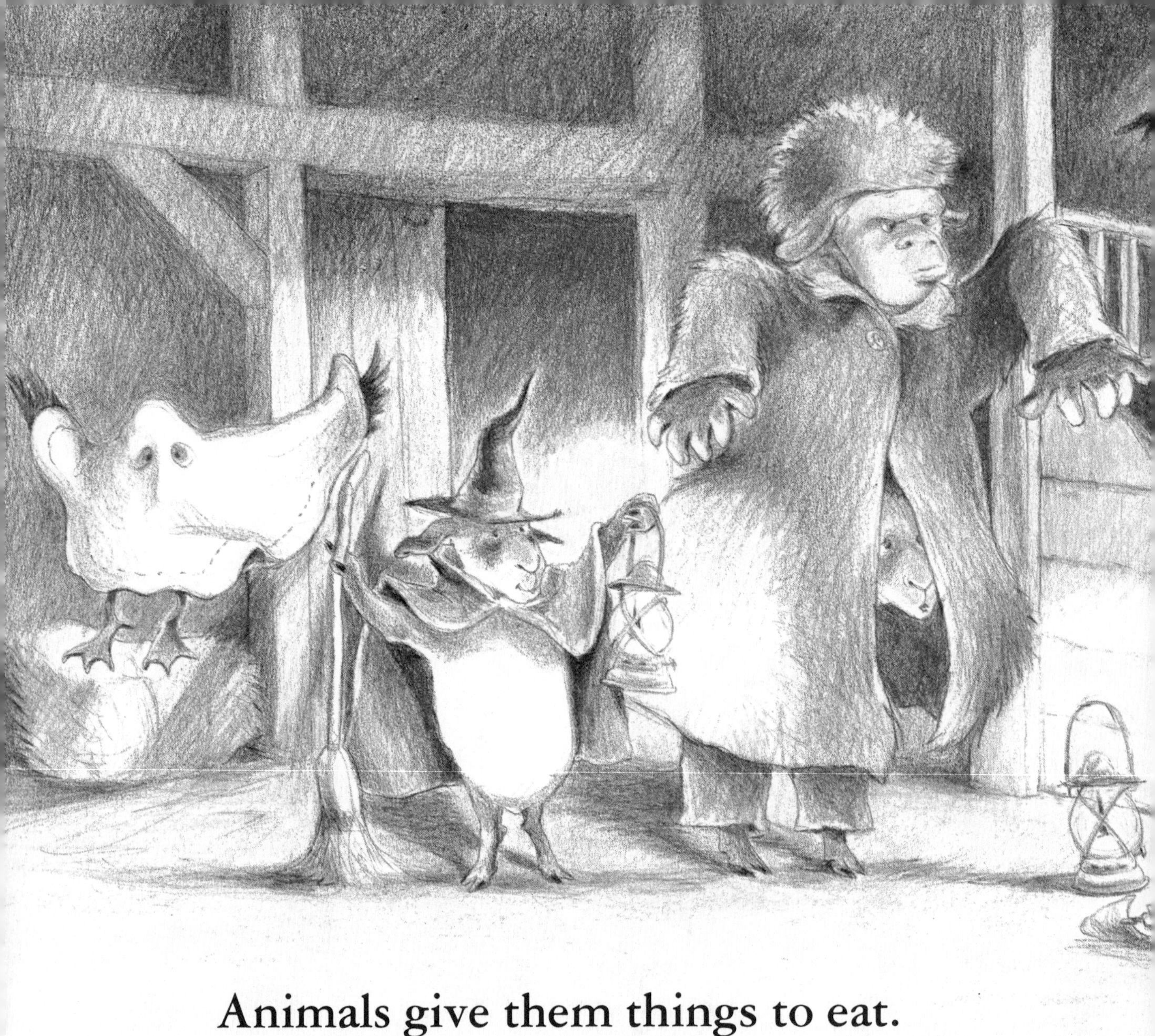

Animals give them things to eat.

The horses' treats go in with thumps:

Apples, oats, and sugar lumps.

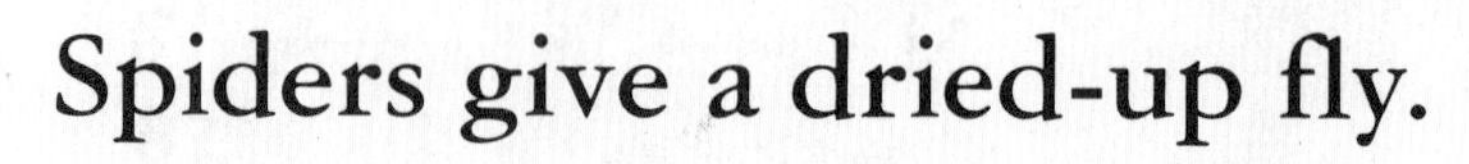

Spiders give a dried-up fly.

Sheep decide to pass it by.

Sheep stop by the chicken coops.

Chickens give them fresh eggs. Oops!

Cows offer hay and clover.

Now the trick-or-treating's over.

Back through the woods the sheep parade.

It’s dark, but they are not afraid.

Rustling noises come from trees.

Is someone there, or just a breeze?

Wolves peek out from hiding places.

Wolves see scary lit-up faces.

Wolves skedaddle.

Sheep skip past.

They settle down with treats at last.